I Fooled You

Ten Stories of Tricks, Jokes, and Switcheroos

collected and edited by Johanna Hurwitz

Introduction copyright © 2010 by Johanna Hurwitz
Compilation copyright © 2010 by Johanna Hurwitz
"Tall Tale" copyright © 2010 by Douglas Florian
"Judy Moody, Stink, and the Super-Sneaky Switcheroo" copyright © 2010 by Megan McDonald
Judy Moody®. Judy Moody is a registered trademark of Candlewick Press, Inc.
"I'm Not James" copyright © 2010 by David A. Adler
"Big Z, Cammi, and Me" copyright © 2010 by Carmela A. Martino
"Poetic Justice" copyright © 2010 by Eve B. Feldman
"April Thirty-first" copyright © 2010 by Johanna Hurwitz
"Sam and Pam" copyright © 2010 by Matthew Holm
"Sweetie Bird" copyright © 2010 by Barbara Ann Porte
"The Bridge to Highlandsville" copyright © 2010 by Michelle Knudsen
"The Prince of Humbugs" copyright © 2010 by Ellen Klages

First edition 2010

Library of Congress Cataloging-in-Publication Data

I fooled you : ten stories of tricks, jokes, and switcheroos / edited and collected by Johanna Hurwitz. — 1st ed.
p. cm.
Contents: Tall tale / Douglas Florian—Judy Moody, Stink, and the super-sneaky switcheroo / Megan McDonald—I'm not James / David A. Adler—Big Z, Cammi, and me / Carmela A. Martino—Poetice justice / Eve Feldman—April 31st / Johanna Hurwitz—Sam and Pam / Matthew Holm—Sweetie bird / Barbara Ann Porte—The bridge to Highlandsville / Michelle Knudsen—The prince of humbugs / Ellen Klages.
ISBN 978-0-7636-3789-7 (hardcover)
ISBN 978-0-7636-4877-0 (paperback)
1. Children's stories, American. 2. Tricks—Juvenile fiction.
3. Practical jokes—Juvenile fiction. [1. Short stories. 2. Tricks—Fiction.
3. Practical jokes—Fiction.] I. Hurwitz, Johanna. II. Title.
PZ5.I215 2010
[Fic]—dc22   2009026017

09 10 11 12 13 14 MVP 10 9 8 7 6 5 4 3 2 1

Printed in York, PA, U.S.A.

This book was typeset in Lucida.

Candlewick Press
99 Dover Street
Somerville, Massachusetts 02144

visit us at www.candlewick.com

To all our readers.
No fooling!

Contents

• • •

Introduction

• • •

Some years ago, I got the idea of putting together a book of short stories by different children's book authors. Wouldn't it be interesting, I thought, to see what would happen if everyone was asked to write about the same premise? I was certain that no two stories would be the same. The book, *Birthday Surprises,* proved me right. Despite the same features in the plots, each author brought an original voice and slant to his or her tale.

It worked once. Would it work again? I thought long and hard in search of another premise, one that would surprise my readers and intrigue the authors who participated in the collection. In discussion with editor Sarah Ketchersid, we came up with the phrase "I fooled you." Each author was asked to include this sentence in his or her story. The results showed that my first anthology was not a fluke. Here again are ten stories that are totally different despite the common element in each one.

A few weeks after sending out requests for stories but before any actually arrived, I woke one morning with a revelation. By selecting the phrase "I fooled you," I was not really being original at all; I was reinventing the wheel. Just about every folk and fairy tale—*Aesop's Fables, The Arabian Nights,* the Uncle Remus stories, and many other classic children's books—contain the act of fooling someone. The sentence

"I fooled you" may not necessarily be included in the story, but it is implied.

Think about it: "Hansel and Gretel" begins with the stepmother plotting to fool the children she plans to lose in the forest. But Hansel fools the stepmother after he overhears her scheming and slips outdoors and fills his pockets with pebbles. He drops these along the route the next day so that he and Gretel can find their way home. That night, the stepmother fools Hansel by locking the door so he can't get a new supply of pebbles. He then uses breadcrumbs instead, but they are eaten by birds. Lost in the woods, Hansel and Gretel find the witch's house, built of cakes, cookies, and candies to fool lost children, whom she then captures to eat. But in the end, the biggest "I fooled you" is played out by Hansel when he is encaged and lets the witch feel a twig, which she thinks is his finger. It's so skinny that she continues to feed him in hopes of fattening him up. In the end, of course, Hansel is triumphant when he pushes the witch into the oven in which she had planned to roast him.

Similarly, tricks are played on the bad guy—be it witch, wolf, ogre, elf, or troll—in "The Three Little Pigs," "Little Red Riding Hood," "Snow White and the Seven Dwarves," "Rumpelstiltskin," "The Three Billy Goats Gruff," and many others. Even the most famous book for children from the nineteenth century, *Alice's Adventures in Wonderland,* is an "I fooled you" story, because author Lewis Carroll reveals to us that it was all a dream. He fooled us! And more recently, Maurice Sendak's *Where the Wild Things Are* also turns out to be an act of Max's imagination and not some exotic kingdom ruled by fantastic creatures. He fooled us, too.

Think about it. I bet you'll come up with other examples where "I fooled you" is a part of the story. And of course, sit down and read the stories included here. I hope you enjoy them all. No fooling!

Johanna Hurwitz

Tall Tale

· · · · · · · · · · · · · · · · ·

DOUGLAS FLORIAN

I was born
in Timbuktu,
was raised by wolves
from Kathmandu.
I sailed with pirates
on high seas
who taught me
French and Japanese.
I trained ten tigers,
wrestled bears;
I rode giraffes

while juggling chairs.
I hung from airplanes
upside down,
then joined the circus
as a clown.
I dug for gold.
I dived for pearls.
I dined with kings
and queens and earls.
I wrote ten plays,
four hundred books.
I gave gorillas
dirty looks.
I climbed high mountains,
swallowed lakes;
I baked a million
chocolate cakes.

I swam across
the English Channel

in my long
underwear of flannel.
I also won
the Super Bowl
(I kicked a
ninety-yard field goal).
And in the famed
Kentucky Derby
I rode the winning horse,
named Herbie.
I paddled down
the Amazon
with William Tell
and Genghis Khan.
I skipped the sixth
and seventh grade
and led the
Labor Day parade.
I ate one hundred
ice-cream cones,

discovered stegosaurus bones.
I carried hippos
piggyback,
then traveled to
the moon and back.

And if you think
all this is true,
then I'll confess that
I fooled you!

Judy Moody, Stink, and the Super-Sneaky Switcheroo

MEGAN McDONALD

It was true. Judy Moody had been playing tricks and jokes and pranks on Stink for as long as he had been her little brother. For sure and absolute positive.

There was the time she faked him out over a so-called moon rock. There was the time she tricked him into picking up a toad and he became an instant member of the Toad Pee Club. And who could forget the best-ever, fake-hand-in-the-toilet trick?

Yep, in the seven short years that Stink had been Judy's little brother, she had (a) turned him into a carrot (with orange hair gel!), (b) taken his dried-up baby belly button to school for Share and Tell, and (c) sent his classroom pet newt down the drain.

That was the long and short of it. The A-B-C of it. She, Judy Moody, ultimate Princess of Pranks, was in a Big Fat Fake-Out Mood. It had been too long since she'd played a joke on Stink and gotten away with it. It was time. Time to get him, and get him good. But how? Judy hadn't even thought up a brainy idea yet. It was still just a germ, a seed inside her, a teeny-tiny speck of genius waiting to grow.

So when Mom asked, "Where's Stink?" Judy was only half listening.

"Where do you think? He's outside watching dirt grow. As usual."

Dad looked up from the splinter he was digging out of his thumb. "He's out babysitting—"

"No fair!" said Judy, sitting up at full attention now. "You said I'm not old enough to babysit yet, and Stink's a year younger than me."

"I was going to say, babysitting his *tomato plants* in the garden," said Dad.

"Oh," said Judy. She went over to the sink and stood on tiptoe to peer out the window. "What's with all the squirt guns?"

"It's for the Science Olympics at school," said Mom.

"I thought he was going to test the effects of baby powder and baking soda on smelly sneakers," said Judy.

"He changed his mind," said Dad. "Now it's something about strangle weed."

"And witches' shoelaces," said Mom.

"Witches' shoelaces! Rare!" said Judy. "This I gotta hear!"

Judy ran outside to the garden. She saw three rows of gangly tomato plants, held up with stakes that looked like rulers or paint stirrers. The tomato plants were covered with weeny green tomatoes, but Judy did not see one red one.

Stink was on all fours, sprinkling Magic Gro around his plants and sniffing the dirt here, there, and everywhere.

"What's up, Stinkerbell?" Judy asked.

"Shh! Can't you see I'm smelling?"

"And you can't smell when I'm talking because . . . ?"

"Sniff right here," said Stink. "Do you smell lemon? Or pineapple?"

Judy took a whiff. "I smell dirt. Plain old yucky everyday dirty dirt."

"You're no help," said Stink. "See, I'm trying to change the smell of these tomato plants."

"Don't you like the smell?" asked Judy. "They sure smell good to me."

"No," said Stink. "Because of dodders."

"What's a dodder?"

"Let's just say there are no good dodders."

"I'm a good daughter," said Judy, cracking herself up. "Ask Mom and Dad."

"Hardee-har-har," said Stink. "Not that kind of dodder. A dodder is an evil weed. A tangly, strangly vine that can actually *smell* a tomato plant. When it smells a tomato growing, it creeps up real sneaky-like and twists all over the plant like spaghetti, then strangles it. That's why they call it strangle weed. Or witches' shoelaces."

"Cool," said Judy, shivering.

"It is so *not* cool," said Stink. "If dodders strangle all these tomato plants, all the green tomatoes will get choked out and I'll never grow a single solitary red ripe tomato."

"But just think, Stink. At least you'll grow a bunch of spaghetti plants. That's way cooler. You could win the Spaghetti Olympics."

"Yeah, right," said Stink. "And flunk the Science Olympics big-time. See, my idea is if I spray these plants with lemon and peppermint and stuff, the evil dodders won't know it's a tomato, and they won't strangle it to death."

"Wouldn't it be easier just to yank up all the witchy weeds?" Judy asked.

"Yeah," said Stink, "if I want to *live* out here in the garden twenty-four seven. They're super sneaky. They just keep growing back.

This way, I'll trick them into thinking these aren't tomato plants. So they'll leave my tomatoes alone. Then pretty soon I'll be taking pictures of all my big fat red ripe monster tomatoes and writing a big fat report about how I saved them."

"Super Tomato Man to the rescue," said Judy. Stink grinned from ear to ear.

"One problem," said Judy. "How are you going to win any Olympics when it takes, like, a million years to grow a red tomato?"

"If I get these guys to quit strangling them, they'll grow super-duper fast. What do you think my trusty-dusty Dodder Busters are for?" said Stink, squirting Judy with two squirt guns at a time.

"Hey!" said Judy, hopping out of the way. "Now I smell like a peppermint pineapple!"

Suddenly, she, Judy Moody, had an idea.

A red ripe idea. A dilly of an idea. A best-ever, fake-out-Stink-for-real idea.

All she needed was a supermarket.

"Since when do you want to go to the super-market?" Mom asked, sounding suspicious.

"Since now," said Judy. "I just wanted to help out. You know, show you how I'm such a good daughter." Judy cracked herself up.

"No, really," said Mom.

"Okay, I'm hungry, and we're all out of frozen corn." Frozen corn was Judy's favorite snack to eat after school.

At the supermarket, Judy hurried and found a great big on-sale bag of frozen corn in the freezer section. And now for the real reason she was there. She tried to look bored, then snuck a bunch more tomatoes into Mom's shopping bag when she wasn't looking. The kind with stems that looked like they just came off the vine.

When Judy got home, she hid the extra tomatoes in her backpack until later.

As soon as it started to get dark, Stink finally came in from Dirt Patrol (aka Dodder Duty). "There are mosquitoes as big as bats out there," said Stink.

"And there are *real* bats out there, too," said Judy. "You better not go back out there anymore tonight." It was Stink's turn to shiver.

Judy waited till Stink went upstairs. She waited till Stink got out his notebook. She waited until Stink was way-far into drawing Tomato-Man-to-the-Rescue comics.

Luckily, Stink was cuckoo for comics, Dad was talking on the phone long-distance, and Mom was reading a murder mystery.

The coast was clear. Nobody would even notice she was gone.

Judy grabbed a flashlight from the kitchen drawer. She snagged a roll of see-through sticky tape and some scissors, too. Then, when nobody was looking, she slipped out the side door into the backyard.

Operation Super-Sneaky Judy Moody versus the Tomato Man was about to begin. And it was going to be the best joke ever. Better than the fake hand in the toilet.

The next morning, Stink came running downstairs in his pajamas. He was all out of breath, and he pointed out the back window. "You—look—see—my—Olympics— overnight—magic—tomatoes!"

"Calm down, Stinkerbell," said Judy.

"Take a breath, Stink," said Dad. "What are you trying to tell us?"

"My tomatoes—the Dodder Buster thing really worked! Yesterday, all I had were puny little weeny green tomatoes that were being strangled out by evil witches' shoelaces. But all of a sudden my tomatoes turned red last night—poof, just like that! Big fat red ripe monster tomatoes. Like magic."

Mom and Dad went over to the window to look.

"Stink, everybody *knows* there's no such *thing* as magic tomatoes," said Judy.

"Ya-huh," said Stink. "See for yourself." He headed for the back door.

Judy ran after Stink. They raced out to the garden in their pajamas. Stink stood back and pointed. "See? Look. Almost every single plant has red ripe tomatoes. Boy, am

I ever going to win the Tomato Olympics."

"Let's get a camera," said Judy. "Take a picture."

"Yeah, let's—" Stink stopped. He squinted. He stooped down to peer closer. "Hey, wait a second. Something's funny. As in fishy. Check this out," said Stink, peering under a leaf. "HEY! These tomatoes aren't magic at all. Somebody just put—"

Judy could not stand it one more minute. Not one more super-sneaky second. "I fooled you, Stinker! Fooled you, fooled you, fooled you!" she sang, jumping up and down.

"Did not!" said Stink.

"Did too!" said Judy. "I got you, Stink Face. Admit it—I got you so good! You thought they were *magic* tomatoes, but really I got them yesterday from the store!"

"Huh?"

"Remember when you came in 'cause you were afraid of bats? I snuck out here with my flashlight when nobody was looking and pulled the greatest-ever big fat tomato switcheroo." Judy laughed herself silly. "Magic tomatoes. Who ever heard of *magic* tomatoes?"

"Hardee-har-har," said Stink. His sister thought she was so funny.

Judy pointed at her little brother. "You should see your face. Your face is as red as a tomato!"

"Ha-ha, very funny," said Stink. "So funny I forgot to laugh."

Stink bent over, picking all the UN-magic tomatoes and collecting them in his stretched-out pajama shirt.

"Stink, don't pick them all. Let's take a picture for real. See, this way you can win the Tomato Olympics for sure."

Stink looked mad. His face was so tomato red, he looked like he was ready to pop! Judy couldn't help laughing some more, just thinking of tomato-head Stink bursting and squirting out tomato juice any second.

"Oh, I'm still going to win the Olympics," said Stink. "Not the Science Olympics. The FOOD FIGHT Olympics! The Tomato *Sauce* Olympics." Stink squished a tomato in his bare hand and tossed it at Judy.

SPLAT!

Zing! Zing! Goosh!

Ick. Ooey, gooey tomato goo was gooshing down the front of Judy's PJ's. Slimy tomato stuff was sliding down her face and yucky-blucky juice and seeds were dripping from her hair.

"Gotcha!" said Stink. "Now *I* fooled *YOU!* Gotcha, gotcha, gotcha," Stink sang back at Judy.

Judy looked around. Stink had picked every last red tomato. She reached for the stash in the front of his pajama shirt.

Goosh! He got her again. "Tomato Man strikes again!" yelled Stink.

But wait. Stink had dropped a few red ripe tomatoes on the ground. Judy scooped one up, squished it in her hand, and yelled, "Stink, you're toast!"

Zing! Tomato slop splattered his arm. She grabbed two more and got him again, one on each leg. Then Judy was all out of tomatoes.

She ran. She ran around the garden and across the yard, zigzagging around trees and hoses and benches and flowerpots.

Stink ran after her. "I might be toast," said Stink. "But you're . . . KETCHUP!"

Zing!

I'm Not James

• • • • • • • • • • • • • • • • • • • •

DAVID A. ADLER

James and I are twins, but we're not identical. Sure we look and talk almost exactly
alike, but we're not the same. He's what Mom
and Dad call a cutup, and I'm not. When
one of my friends is about to sit down, I
don't pull the chair out so he falls to the
floor and then laugh and say, "I fooled you!"
In the cafeteria, I never stapled someone's
drinking straw. But James did.

We were in the third grade, at lunch, and
Elliot was sipping milk between bites of

his cream-cheese-and-jelly sandwich. He took an apple from his lunch bag and saw it was all bruised, so he went to throw it out. And when he came back, James said, "Drink some more milk. It's good for you." Elliot tried, and you already know why he couldn't. James laughed, held up the stapler, and said, "I fooled you!"

Oh, and I wasn't the one who put a phony note in Ms. Tower's mailbox asking her to send Allison to the principal's office. James did. You already know what he said when Allison came back to class all angry: "I fooled you!"

He's done worse stuff, but I can't tell you about most of it because no one but me knows it was James who did it. Let's just say that when the builder started pouring cement for the foundation for a new house down our block and the frame was in the wrong place because someone had moved the wooden stakes, well, I know who moved them. I also know whose hand-prints are in the cement walk. And I know who hid an alarm clock behind the vent in my fifth-grade classroom and set it to go off in the middle of a math test. I just won't say who.

The worst part of my brother's mischief is that if I'm nearby, my friends are afraid to sit on a chair. In the cafeteria, if they walk away, they won't leave their straws in their milk containers. They're never really sure I'm not James. Well, I'm not! I'm George, and since *identical* means exactly alike, and we're not identical twins, that means we're not exactly alike, and if you would take the time to really look at both of us, you'd know that.

First of all, I have a birthmark on my right knee that James doesn't have. It's a not-so-dark spot roughly the shape but not the size of Idaho. It's about an inch and a half across.

When I was in kindergarten and first grade and someone asked which twin I was, I just pulled up my pant leg and showed him Idaho. Now that I'm in sixth grade, I mostly wear jeans. Did you ever try pulling a denim pant leg over your knee? Well, you can't, and anyway, I think it's kinda gross to show people my knee anytime I want them to know who I am.

For about two weeks in third grade, I had a better way to let people know I'm George. That's because some man named Raymond George was running for mayor. Well, I got one of his campaign buttons—a blue one with a big red GEORGE on it—and I wore it to school. It was great. People saw it and knew I was the good twin. Like I said, that only worked for two weeks. After that, James got a GEORGE button and wore it, too. By the way, Raymond George was elected and I'm sorry I wore his button. He's one of those "education mayors" and because of him our school vacations are shorter.

When we were in lower school, there were just two classes in each grade. After kindergarten, James and I were never in the same class, but any time we took a trip or were at recess, there he was. He'd do some mischief and sometimes I'd get in trouble for it. Well, this year we started middle school and there are lots more classes, so I don't see him as much. That's the good part. The bad part is, not everyone knows there are two of us.

Like yesterday.

Mrs. Baylor — she's the cafeteria teacher — left her books and whistle on the chair by the line-up place. It was just the beginning of lunch, and she was talking to another teacher. When her back was turned, James tore off a corner of a ketchup packet and squeezed some into the part of her whistle where the bouncing little metal ball makes all the noise. Well, Mrs. Baylor finished talking before James finished squeezing. She turned and saw what he was doing. She ran to her whistle, and James ran into the crowd of kids waiting in line for food.

What happened next was really funny.

Mrs. Baylor grabbed the whistle, wiped it with a tissue, and then blew into it. No noise came out, but ketchup did. It looked like the whistle was bleeding, and it bled onto the front of her shirt.

Mrs. Baylor threw the whistle down and looked for James. She looked right at the line of kids waiting for lunch and grabbed me. "You'll wish you never did that!" she hollered.

"But I didn't do it!"

She grabbed my arm and pulled me through the halls, and I could tell she was really angry. Her face was red and she squeezed my arm so hard, I could feel her fingernails digging into my skin.

"You've ruined my shirt!" she told me as we passed the gym.

"But you've got the wrong boy. I'm a twin."

"You'll wish you never saw a ketchup packet!"

Who ever wastes wishes on ketchup packets?

"Just you wait! Mr. Simmons won't think this is funny!"

She was right about that. Mr. Simmons is the principal and he doesn't think anything is funny.

She pulled me into the main office. "I've got to see Mr. Simmons," she told the woman behind the desk.

"He's with a parent."

Mrs. Baylor tapped on the desk, a sort of rhythmic tune. The beat quickened. She was getting impatient.

"I need some paper."

The woman behind the desk gave her a sheet of paper. Mrs. Baylor took a pencil from the cup on the desk and started to write, but she pressed so hard, the pencil point broke. She took another pencil and wrote some more. She wrote half a page, gave it to the woman, pointed to me, and said, "This is the boy."

"No, I'm not," I protested.

"Don't listen to him. Just look at my shirt. Ketchup," she said, and pointed to a large red spot right where her heart should be. "I saw him squeeze ketchup into my whistle. I want this boy punished."

With that she marched out of the office.

I watched the woman behind the desk read the note. She smiled. I guess blowing into a whistle filled with ketchup is funny if you're not the one blowing into the whistle or the one blamed for it.

"This is a big mistake," I told her. "I'm a twin and Mrs. Baylor got the wrong one."

"I'm sorry," she said, "but you'll have to wait for Mr. Simmons."

I sat there and waited.

"I'm hungry," I told the woman behind the desk. "I didn't get to eat my lunch."

"I'm sorry," she said again, but I'm not sure she was.

When Mr. Simmons and the parent he was meeting with—someone's mother—came out of his office, I knew this would not go well for me. Neither of them looked happy.

"I'm sure this will all work out," Mr. Simmons said. But he didn't look sure and the mother didn't seem reassured. She just nodded solemnly and left.

The woman behind the desk gave Mr. Simmons the note. He read it, glared at me, and said, "James, this isn't funny."

When people keep saying that about something, that it isn't funny, it probably is. Actually, if I wasn't the one blamed for the bleeding whistle, I would probably be laughing.

"I'm not James," I told him. "I'm George. Mrs. Baylor got the wrong twin."

"Mrs. Baylor wrote that she saw you with the ketchup packet and grabbed you."

"Here," I said. "Look!"

I took the math quiz from my pocket. I pointed to the name at the top of the paper and said, "I'm George."

Mr. Simmons softened a bit and said, "If it was your brother, he'd be in real trouble. I've had just about enough of his mischief. But since it's you, I'll just keep you here until the end of the day."

"But—" I started to say. Then I stopped. I didn't want James to get into real trouble. I didn't want him thrown out of school. I just wished someone would teach him a lesson.

I sat there until the end of the school day. I missed my last three classes—history, science, and gym. I had nothing to do but sit there, watch kids and teachers come in and out of the office, and listen to my stomach growl. I was bored and hungry.

I had plenty of time to think.

I decided I was the one to teach James a lesson. But how?

When I got home, I talked to him, and do you know what? He wanted *me* to thank *him.*

"I got you out of history," he said. "That Mrs. Heller is a real witch."

"No!" I shouted. "I won't thank you and the next time you get me in trouble with the principal, I won't save you. I'll show him Idaho and you'll be thrown out of school."

James is wrong about Mrs. Heller. She's not a witch. She's just a serious teacher. We both have her, but not the same period, and we both had to study for a history test the next day.

I studied. James tried. But he gets distracted. While I was reading about Calvin Coolidge and the Roaring Twenties, he was doodling. While I was suffering through the Great Depression, he was eating Froot Loops.

I took the test during sixth period. James had it earlier, before lunch. I thought the test was easy. James was sure he failed.

On Thursday Mrs. Heller handed back our tests. I did great. James failed. At lunch-time, he was sullen.

"This is it," he told me. "Mrs. Heller is letting me take another test on that stuff and if I don't pass, she's going to Mr. Simmons. She said I may even have to go to summer school."

Wow!

"I'm studying tonight. I'm going to work at it. I don't want to sit in some dumb school all summer."

I was surprised. That night, he really did

study. He had me ask him the questions at the end of the chapter, and he knew the work. I was sure he would do well on the test.

I was in the front hall the next morning when Mrs. Heller came up to me.

"Follow me," she said.

I followed her.

"I don't have a class first period," she said when we got to her room. "You'll have plenty of time to take the test."

"But—"

"There will be no buts and no fooling around," she told me. "This is your chance to redeem yourself."

She gave me the test. It was different from the one we had earlier in the week. There were just twenty questions. I looked at the test and told myself, *This is it! This is my chance to teach James a lesson.*

Question one: *What was the Eighteenth Amendment to the Constitution. How did it change society?*

Mrs. Heller talked about that a lot. It made it against the law to sell or drink liquor, but that's not what I answered.

I wrote: *The eighteenth amendment is a sundae with eighteen almonds—almonds were once called amendments—lots of strawberry syrup, and it's not good for your constitution because it upsets your stomach.*

Question two: *Who was known as "Silent Cal"?*

Instead of answering, President Calvin Coolidge, I wrote: *That was Babe Ruth's real name, only nobody knew it because he kept silent about that stuff.*

I smiled. I can be as funny as James, I thought, and when Mrs. Heller tells him he failed the test for the second time and he'll have to go to summer school, I'll just say, "This time I fooled *you!*"

I looked at the third question: *What were some of the causes of the Great Depression?*

I was about to write something about how your clothes get wrinkled if you sleep in them and you greatly need to press them and that's the Great Depression, when I asked myself, *What am I doing? Maybe James would do something like this. Maybe he would think this is funny, but it really isn't. If I hand in this test, I'll be just like James.*

"Mrs. Heller," I said, "I'm not James. I'm George."

At first she didn't believe me. She asked me all sorts of questions, things James wouldn't know because they happened in my class and not in his. At last she was convinced.

I left her room surprisingly pleased. Like I said, James and I are not the same.

I didn't see James at lunch. He was taking Mrs. Heller's test. She marked it right then, and he passed. She told him what had happened in the morning, and when we got home, he thanked me. Then he promised to change, but I'm not sure he meant he would stop his mischief, because right after he said it, he changed his shirt and sneakers. But whatever he meant—whether he'll change his ways or just his clothing—at least I know, like I said before, that James and I are not identical.

Big Z, Cammi, and Me

· · · · · · · · · · · · · · · · ·

CARMELA A. MARTINO

I didn't notice anything wrong at first.

My official Chicago Cubs clock radio woke me as usual. Mom'd given me the radio as a back-to-school present two weeks ago, saying, "Now that you're in sixth grade, Josh, you'll have to get yourself out of bed." No problem. Till today.

When the radio came on, the announcer's voice was immediately drowned out by a loud meow. I opened my eyes to see Big Z standing next to the nightstand. He jumped onto the bed and rubbed his gray-and-black-striped body against my arm. He meowed again, a meow that said, "Feed me NOW."

"All right, Z," I said. "Keep your *pantalones* on." *Pantalones* is Spanish for pants. Of course Big Z never wears anything besides his official Chicago Cubs pet collar. But since I'm taking Spanish this year, I had decided to teach Z, too. That way he can be bilingual, like the Cubs pitcher I named him after—Carlos "Big Z" Zambrano.

I turned off the radio without waiting for the sports update. I already knew that the Cubs had won yesterday's game.

When I got to the kitchen, Big Z was waiting beside the cabinet where we keep the cat food. Mom always buys the economy-size bag—Z's a big eater. I was so groggy that I didn't notice how full the bag was. The Kitty Krunchies came pouring out. They flew everywhere. Not a good way to start a Monday.

Big Z didn't mind, though. He attacked the Krunchies on the floor like he hadn't eaten in days. I hurried to clean up before Mom saw the mess. Lucky for me, she hadn't come down yet. That was strange.

I glanced at the microwave clock, then did a double take. 6:18? How could that be? I'd set my alarm for 6:45.

I scooped the last of the Krunchies into Big Z's bowl and went back to my room. From the doorway, I read the time on my Cubs clock radio: 6:20. Confused, I walked over for a closer look. The rectangular clock is Cubbie blue, except for the big red *C* on top. The radio ON/OFF button sits in the middle of the *C*.

I picked up the clock and checked the alarm—it was still set for 6:45.

As I put the clock back on the nightstand, I tried to replay in my mind exactly what had happened when I woke up. I couldn't remember actually hearing an announcer's voice. Maybe I'd dreamed that the radio woke me. Strange, though. I could've sworn I'd pressed the button to turn it off before going to the kitchen.

Then I thought, *Who cares? I can sleep for twenty more minutes.*

I slept till the radio came on for real at 6:45, just in time for Rigley Fielder's sports update. "Good news for Cubs fans this Monday morning," Fielder said. "The Brewers lost last night, which means the Cubs are now tied with them for first place." All right! With only a few weeks left to the season, the Cubs had a good chance to make the play-offs. I could hardly wait for tonight's game.

After dinner, I put on my official Carlos "Big Z" Zambrano jersey and turned on the TV. Too bad Dad was out of town and couldn't watch with me. Mom thinks baseball is boring, and my kid sister just doesn't get it. At least I had Z to keep me company. He was real excited, too—Carlos Zambrano himself was going to be on the mound for the Cubs.

While Z and I waited for the game to start, we practiced the tricks I'd taught him. Z loves doing tricks, which is pretty cool for a cat. His favorite is high-five. Every time the Cubs score, I put up my hand and say, "*Dame cinco.*" That's Spanish for "give me five." Then Z slaps my hand with his paw. I was hoping to do that a lot tonight.

But after a couple of innings, the game was scoreless. Z must've wandered off, 'cause he wasn't around when Zambrano came to bat in the bottom of the fifth. The score was still tied at zero, with two on and two out.

I clutched my official Cubs souvenir plush baseball for luck. "Come on, Zambrano," I said to the TV. "Get a hit."

Crack. A double!

"Woo-hoo!" I tossed the ball into the air. "He did it, Z. *Dame cinco* time." But Z didn't come when I called.

I searched the house. Upstairs, I noticed that my little sister's bedroom door was closed. Uh-oh.

I knocked. "Cammi, is Big Z in there?"

Through the door, I heard a meow.

I tried the knob. Locked.

"Cammi, let me in." Z meowed louder. "Right now."

Click. The door slowly opened.

Big Z was sitting on Cammi's pink bedspread surrounded by her dolls and stuffed animals. *"Meooww,"* he whined, jumping to the floor. He had something pink and frilly around his middle.

"Geez, Cammi. A tutu?"

"I'm teaching him to dance," Cammi said. "Watch." She dangled a long white ribbon above Z's head. "Dance, Big Z."

Z got up on his hind legs. He stepped from side to side, reaching for the ribbon. Cammi giggled.

"Cut it out," I said. "You're making him look stupid." I grabbed Z, slid the tutu off, and threw it on the floor.

"I wanted to teach him something, too—something special."

"Big Z is *my* cat," I said. "I'm the one who feeds him and cleans out his poop box. That means *I'm* the one who teaches him tricks."

Cammi glared at me. "You were a lot nicer before you started junior high. Now you think you're so smart."

"You're just jealous," I said. "Come on, Z."

As I carried Z back to the family room, I said to him, "After the game, I'll teach you a respectable trick. How about fetch?"

Big Z meowed, and I knew it meant "Sure thing!"

Because of Cammi, Z had missed seeing Zambrano score, but we did our high fives anyway. I laughed. It always tickles a little when Z pats my hand with his paw.

The Cubs ended up winning five to nothing. With the Brewers' loss earlier in the day, the Cubs now had first place all to themselves. Z and I did a few more high fives, just for fun. Then we started working on our new trick. I tossed my Cubs plush baseball across the hardwood floor. "Fetch, Z."

Z ran after the ball. But after he had it in his mouth, he refused to let go. We played tug-of-war for a while. Finally, I offered him a treat and he dropped the ball like a hot tamale. It didn't take Z long to figure out that if he brought the ball back to me after I threw it, I'd give him another treat.

"*Muy bueno,* Z," I said, rubbing him behind the ears. "Very good." All the stuff I'd read about training cats really worked. Maybe I'd teach him to use the toilet next— then I wouldn't have to clean his litter box anymore.

I heard footsteps in the hall and saw

Cammi go by. "Hey, Cammi," I called. "I'm teaching Z a real trick. Wanna see?"

"Can't," Cammi said, her voice flat. "It's my bedtime. I'm not allowed to stay up as late as you."

She was still mad. I didn't understand why. If anyone should be mad, it was me.

When the radio woke me Tuesday morning, I lay waiting for the sports update.

"Meoowww," Big Z whined over a commercial for Kitty Krunchies.

"I'll get your breakfast in a minute," I said.

The announcer's voice came on. "And now, for the traffic report."

"Huh?" I looked at the clock. 6:10. What was going on?

Then I remembered yesterday.

Big Z meowed again.

"Quiet, Z." I picked up the radio. The alarm was still set for 6:45. I pinched myself on the arm. "Ouch." I definitely wasn't dreaming this time.

I heard a toilet flush. My brain suddenly woke up. *Cammi!*

I reached the hallway just as she opened the bathroom door. "Very funny, Cammi."

"What?" Cammi gave me a confused look.

"Don't act so innocent," I said. "You thought you could get away with it again."

"What are you talking about?"

Mom and Dad's bedroom door opened. "What's going on?" Mom said.

"Cammi played a trick on me."

"Did not," Cammi croaked.

"Then why are you up so early?" I said.

"I had to go to the bathroom." She put a hand to her throat. "I don't feel so good."

Mom touched Cammi's forehead.

"Don't fall for it, Mom," I said.

Mom ignored me. "You do feel warm," she said to Cammi. "Go back to bed. I'll get the thermometer."

I stood next to Cammi's bed as Mom took her temperature. "She's faking it, Mom."

"Then explain this." Mom held the thermometer out to me.

I didn't believe it—Cammi had a fever of 101.3!

"My throat really hurts," Cammi said.

"I'll make you some hot tea," Mom said.

I followed Mom to the kitchen. "Okay, maybe she *is* sick," I said. "That doesn't prove she didn't sneak into my room and turn on my radio."

"Why would she do that, Josh?"

"She's mad 'cause I won't let her teach Big Z a trick."

Big Z meowed at his name. He was standing beside his empty bowl.

"He looks hungry," Mom said.

"He's always hungry." I filled his bowl while Mom put the teakettle on.

"Aren't you going to punish Cammi?" I said.

"Of course not," Mom said. "You must have accidentally set your alarm for the wrong time."

"But I didn't," I said. "I checked."

"There has to be some other explanation," Mom said. "We'll figure it out later. Go back to bed now, Josh."

Mom always took Cammi's side, just 'cause she's younger. I had to find a way to prove what Cammi had done.

When I got home from school, I found out that Cammi had strep throat. Mom was making her stay in bed till her fever went away.

I didn't care how sick she was—I didn't trust Cammi not to trick me again. She had the perfect alibi now. So I set a trap. I took out my official Cubs collectible miniature baseball bats, all twelve of them, and arranged them on the floor alongside my bed. If Cammi tried to get to my clock radio while I was asleep, she'd get caught in my trap. Then I'd have my proof.

When the radio woke me Wednesday morning, I checked the time right away. 6:45. Good. Either Cammi had been too sick to bother me or she was waiting to catch me off guard. It didn't matter. I was ready for her.

I leaned on my elbow and waited to hear if the Cubs had won last night. They'd had a late West Coast game, and I'd tried to convince Mom to let me stay up for the end. After all, I was in junior high now. I deserved a few more privileges. But she'd said no and threatened to take away my TV rights altogether if I didn't go to bed.

"The seesaw battle in the National League Central Division continues," Rigley Fielder said. "Last night's game lasted twelve innings, with the Cubs finally losing eleven to ten. They're now tied for first place with the Brewers again."

Darn!

"Why the sad face?" Mom asked when I reached the kitchen. She was holding a steaming mug.

"Cubs lost."

"Too bad," she said, but she didn't sound very sincere. "I'm going to bring your sister some tea. Would you like some?"

I shook my head. Did she think a cup of tea would cheer me up?

I went to the cabinet to get Big Z's breakfast. Funny, he didn't come at the sound of the Kitty Krunchies clattering into his bowl.

"Big Z, where are you?" I walked upstairs to look for him. As I reached the top step, Cammi's bedroom door opened. Mom came out, followed by Big Z. "Hey," I said, "what was Z doing in there?"

"Cammi begged me to let him sleep with her," Mom said. "I didn't think you'd mind."

"Well, I do mind. You won't let me stay up to watch an important game, but you give Cammi whatever she wants."

"Have a heart, Josh," Mom said. "She's not feeling well."

"She felt well enough to play a trick on me yesterday."

"I don't believe that," Mom said. "Your clock must be defective."

I shook my head. No sense arguing with Mom. She'd see I was right when I caught Cammi in my trap.

That night, before getting into bed, I brought Big Z to my room and shut the door. He was sleeping with *me* tonight. I carefully stepped around my miniature-baseball-bat trap and climbed into bed.

I was so tired when the clock radio went off the next morning, I couldn't open my eyes. The announcer said, "Good morning, Chicago. After the news, we'll have the latest on a landmark study of animal intelligence. But first, here's news at the top of the hour."

"What?" My eyes popped open. The clock read 6:00! Not again.

"Meoww!" I looked down and saw Big Z standing with his paws between my minia-ture baseball bats. The bats were stacked just as I'd left them. How had Cammi man-aged to get to the radio without tripping?

I turned off the radio. Big Z meowed again.

"Shh, Z. I've got a score to settle." I walked across the hall to Cammi's room. Listening through her door, I heard snoring. What a faker.

I opened the door and tiptoed to the bed. I bent over, ready to scream in her ear. Then I stopped. Cammi was clutching her purple stuffed kitten, the one she calls Baby Z, under her chin. Her face had that sweet-little-kid look she only gets when she's sound asleep.

I whispered, "Cammi, are you awake?"

Her snoring didn't miss a beat. Either she'd suddenly morphed into the next great child actress or I was wrong about her.

I hurried back to check my clock. As I entered my room, my foot caught on something. I fell to the floor with a *thud*. A miniature baseball bat smacked me in the shoulder. "Ouch." I'd tripped on my own trap.

"Meow," Z said from above my head.

"I know," I said, rubbing my shoulder. "I look really *estúpido."*

I stood and picked up my clock. The alarm was still set for 6:45. Somehow, I wasn't surprised. Maybe Mom was right—the clock *was* defective. But why did it take two weeks to start acting strange?

As I put the clock back onto the nightstand, I accidentally pressed the radio ON/OFF button. The announcer said, "The animal study was conducted at the University of Chicago—"

Big Z's "feed me now" meow drowned out the voice.

"It's too early for breakfast, Z." I turned off the radio and plopped onto my bed.

I'd just shut my eyes when I heard a soft *thump.* I opened my eyes. There, standing on the nightstand, was Big Z. He reached over and placed his paw on top of the clock, right over the radio ON/OFF button. The announcer's voice came on again. "... domesticated cats have greater reasoning abilities than previously suspected."

"It was *you,* Z." I sat upright. "*You* tricked me. Not Cammi."

Big Z jumped from the nightstand onto my bed. *"Meow,"* he demanded again, rubbing his body against my arm.

"You wanted to be fed, and you couldn't wait," I said, thinking out loud. "You must've noticed that I always feed you when the radio comes on. So you figured out how to turn it on yourself." I grabbed Z and looked him in the eyes. "I thought I was teaching *you* tricks. But you were the one training me."

This time, when Big Z meowed, I knew it meant "I fooled you!" And that meant Cammi was right—I wasn't as smart as I thought. I owed her a big apology.

I wonder how you say "I'm sorry" in Spanish.

Poetic Justice

· · · · · · · · · · · · · · · · · ·

EVE B. FELDMAN

Someday, I'm going to write a book called *Highly Successful People Who Weren't the Greatest Students.* I could dedicate it to myself. Just kidding! I'm not sure, but I think Albert Einstein and Ben Franklin weren't necessarily their teachers' favorite students. And there was some story about Bill Gates, although I think he did go to Harvard for a while. So maybe there's hope for me.

And when I'm really important and pow-erful, I'll campaign to do away with home-work. (It would be great if I could just declare a law like that, but I'm not plan-ning on becoming a dictator.) I'll explain that kids need time to relax, breathe, and explore, and that homework cuts into that way too much.

I can't say I was ever really a model stu-dent. Maybe, in kindergarten, I was the kind of kid that teachers liked, or at least didn't dislike. Maybe I did what I was told without staring off into space. And I probably didn't get into trouble for not doing homework. I don't remember the kind of homework that we might have had in kindergarten. Cut-ting out pictures from magazines to show the sounds of various letters? I can vaguely remember doing that. I think I recall some kind of workbook pages, too. But even back then, I thought homework was a dumb idea. I had more important stuff to do. Riding bikes, playing ball, playing on the computer, teasing my sisters—anything seemed more important than homework. I wasn't going to waste time drawing lines between words or coloring in a picture. I've always hated coloring in.

Every year, my no-homework habit has seemed to irritate my teachers more and more. I would read the books for a book report but I refused to do some of the presentation stuff, like making a diorama or dressing up as one of the characters. It just wasn't me. This led to a few—all right, a lot of—arguments with teachers and my parents. But by fifth grade, my reputation was established. "Noncompliant" was a term I heard a lot. "Not living up to his potential."

So, I have no idea what made me want to do the assignment we had in the beginning of April in fifth grade. We were supposed to write a poem about a season. Everyone in the room seemed to be busy choosing winter, spring, or summer. The pro-winter people were talking about how they loved snow and snow days and the major holidays that were all winter holidays. Others were looking forward to the warmth of spring, with tweeting birds and blooming flowers. Pete, Joaquin, and Lou all said they only liked summer because it meant baseball and no school. I didn't hear anyone say a word about the fourth season, autumn. I guess I like being different, so I thought I might just give it a try. It seemed like at least I'd stand out as the only guy writing about fall.

That night, after some forced daydreaming about autumn, I felt like I really remembered what it was like. (If there were a
report-card grade for daydreaming, I'd always
get an A in that.) I could picture the green
leaves turning orange, yellow, and red and
how they'd drift down slowly, sometimes
in what seemed like slow motion and other
times in a swirl. I could remember the
crunch of the leaves under my feet and the
perfect weather of fall. But then I pictured
how it ended, with the trees looking like
something you'd see in the beginning of a
really sad movie, or even a horror film. So,
I sat down and started my poem.

The next day, Ms. Marks seemed surprised
that I was handing in something. I had a
feeling that she'd be even more surprised
when she read it. I'd shown off a bit, using

some impressive words and some poetry words, too, like the word *o'er.*

A few days later, Ms. Marks handed back our season poems and had some kids read theirs to the class. Al's was great. It had the crack of the bat and the sound of the waves of summer. He even mentioned arguing with his mom about sunscreen.

I raised my hand. "I didn't get mine back," I said.

"See me after class, Oliver," she said.

So there I was at her desk, imagining great things. *"We've entered your poem in a statewide contest. We're submitting your poem to a magazine. I'm so glad to see that you've broken your no-homework attitude and handed in such a fine, original, thoughtful poem."* Those were just some of the mild compliments I expected to hear. I stood by her desk patiently, grinning proudly.

Ms. Marks handed me my paper, with a big zero on it and a note written in red, "See me after class."

I was stunned. "Didn't you think it was a good poem?" I asked.

"It's an incredibly good poem," she said. "That's why I know you didn't write it. I don't know where you copied it from or who wrote it for you, but it's obviously not yours."

I felt my face getting hot. "But it's mine, all mine," I said. "Every single word of it."

"Think this over carefully, Oliver. I'll be calling your parents this evening. We'll set up a meeting and you can explain yourself then. Remember, we must always face the consequences of our actions."

"There's nothing to explain, Ms. Marks," I said. "This is my work."

"We'll discuss it at a meeting with your parents. It will be better if you admit what you've done," was all she said.

I left the classroom and the building in a daze. Of course, I didn't cry, but my eyes were full of some liquid and felt like they wanted to let it out.

My sister Nellie was home and instantly saw that I was upset. I told her what had happened.

"Tell me the truth, Oliver: did you copy a poem from somewhere?"

"Absolutely not. I wrote the whole thing myself!" I practically shouted.

"Show me the poem," said Nellie. I unzipped my book bag and handed it to her.

"Wow, this is good," she said. She started reading it aloud. "'Autumn is here / when summer is gone and winter is near. / Autumn's attire is of colors so bright, / spreading o'er the world friendship and light.'"

I recited the next lines from memory. "'But autumn is dressed for a last fling at life, / quietly submitting without any strife. / So each leaf, be it large or small, / must quietly change, and then must fall.'"

"It is impressive," said Nellie. "I mean it's great. But let's face it, Oli, you're not known as someone who does his homework almost ever, and this is, like, incredible."

"So you don't believe me either?" I said. My own sister didn't think I had it in me to write a great poem. I sighed heavily, thinking I couldn't expect much better treatment from my parents.

Dinner was awful. I don't even remember what the food was, but Ms. Marks had already spoken to my father. My parents looked even more tired and stressed than usual. Only my two younger sisters ate as if nothing were wrong.

Before the evening was over, each of my parents had pulled me aside for a private chat.

"Why don't you just get a lie detector?" I asked my father.

"Calm down, Oli," said my father. "We're on your side."

"Admit it, Dad," I said. "Even you have your doubts."

My father insisted that he believed me, but I had trouble believing *him.* And my mother just hugged me and said, "You may not have been the most hardworking student, Oli, but you're smart and honest and full of talent. We'll see this through."

The meeting was the next morning in the principal's office. A sub filled in for Ms. Marks in our classroom so that she could join the principal, the school psychologist, my parents, and me as we filed into the teachers' conference room. I hoped that my classmates didn't know that I was about to go on trial for fraud.

Everyone shook hands, and then Ms. Marks produced the evidence, my poem. "I haven't found where you copied this from," she said, "but it's only a matter of time. The Internet is a great detective tool for teachers uncovering cheaters."

"I'm not a cheater," I blurted out.

"Calm down, son," said my father, looking particularly uncalm himself. "The school has promised to hear from us and from you."

The evidence against me was pretty straightforward. "Oliver Gallo has a reputation of doing minimal work in his classes and rarely handing in homework," Ms. Marks said. "He is polite and seems capable, doing well enough on tests and surprisingly well on standardized tests. He is not a discipline problem but daydreams frequently and is certainly not living up to his potential."

The poem, exhibit A, if this was a real trial, was read aloud.

"Dr. Banks," I said to the principal, when it was my turn to speak, "I can recite the poem by heart, because I wrote every word of it myself."

"I'm sorry, but that is no defense," said Ms. Marks. "You could easily have copied it and then memorized it. This meeting will be much better for you if you confess and cite your true sources. Just admit that you cheated and you thought you could fool us."

I looked around the room. My parents looked at me lovingly but anxiously. The principal looked at me expectantly. Ms. Marks looked like a lawyer on one of those lawyer TV shows, at the part where the prosecutor looks satisfied and convinced of a win. The psychologist looked like a juror.

I looked around at every one of them and decided it was all up to me. I had to speak honestly and clear this mess up before it got worse. I felt like saying, "Ladies and gentlemen of the jury," but I knew that would only make it more difficult.

"I confess," I said, and I saw my parents

go white and breathe in sharply as my father put his hand over my mother's. "I confess that I fooled you, but not the way you think. I wrote every word of that poem myself. I fooled you into thinking that I wasn't capable of hard work and home-work. You had no reason to think that I could do what I can do, because I never allowed you to know that I could. I'm sorry that I fooled you, because it ended up hurt-ing me and my family for no good reason."

My parents stood up and hugged me. The principal conferred with the psy-chologist and Ms. Marks. Ms. Marks still didn't seem convinced and said that she thought, sooner or later, she'd find the origin of my original poem. I knew she wouldn't—couldn't—so I wasn't worried about that. I did wonder if I could ever feel comfortable in her class again or if she'd be happy if I went back to the classroom as if nothing had happened.

The case was closed. I wasn't sure what would happen next, but I knew I'd have to stop fooling around, at least some of the time.

April Thirty-first

• • • • • • • • • • • • • • • • • • •

JOHANNA HURWITZ

A week ago Friday, I was so mad, I couldn't
pay attention in class.

"Mimi, what is the answer to the next
question?" my fifth-grade teacher asked.

I startled alert, but although the social-
studies quiz was on my desk, right in front
of me, I had no idea which was the next
question.

"What one is that?" I asked, feeling my
face turn red.

"Mimi. It will be the weekend soon enough. Try to stay with us for now," Mrs. Howard said. She turned her head and called on another student.

I tried to follow the class discussion, but within moments my mind had wandered again. Sitting two rows in front of me was Sandy Kolman. She was wearing a pair of plaid pants and a matching vest. There was a bright pink stripe in the plaid, and her shirt was exactly the same shade of pink. I couldn't take my eyes off of her. Last year that outfit belonged to me.

How would you feel if every time you looked at someone they were wearing your old clothes? I know she gets almost everything she owns from Twice Blessed. That's a nonprofit thrift shop in town that raises money for cancer research. My mom brings bags of stuff there all the time. I tried to get her to just throw my outgrown clothing in the garbage. "Or find another place to take it," I said last week. "It's awful seeing someone wearing my stuff."

"Mimi. Get a life," my mother said.

"What's that supposed to mean?" I asked.

"I mean, you shouldn't be obsessed about your old clothing. You have lots of new things to wear and if someone can get use out of items you've outgrown, great. And if it raises money for charity, too, so much the better."

It's easy for her to say. She's not growing and changing sizes the way I am. So it's *my* clothing that goes to Twice Blessed. And every time Sandy Kolman walks into class, I feel twice cursed. There she is, dressed in my old stuff.

I wished I could talk with my grand-mother. She always understood me, and she could always make me feel better when I was upset. The horrible thing is that my grandmother is alive and not alive. She has Alzheimer's disease, which means her memory is gone. She lives in a special residence now and not in her own apartment. When we go to visit her, she just stares at us, trying to remember who we are. Last week she called me Trudy. Who is Trudy? Even my mother couldn't guess. A friend from her childhood? A cousin who died young? A neighbor who moved away?

Somehow I got through the day at school. But in between activities, I thought about my grandmother, who no longer knew who I was, and Sandy Kolman, who looked like me a year ago. My grandmother had always admired that plaid outfit. If she saw Sandy, would she call her Mimi?

On Saturday, Adele Cummings came over to my house. We've been friends since kindergarten. Our teachers always work hard to separate us during the school day, putting us on different committees and in different study groups. But outside of school, we're together all the time, starting in the morning, when we sit together on the school bus, then at lunch, when we eat side by side in the cafeteria, and in the afternoons, when we go to the same ballet class and swimming lessons.

"What do you make of Sandy Kolman?" I asked Adele.

"What do you mean?" she said.

"Well, what do you think of her?" I asked again.

She shrugged. "I've never gotten to know her very well," she said finally. "All I know about her is what you know. She moved to town when we were in the middle of third grade. She lives with her mother and her younger sister in one of those apartment buildings on the edge of town and not in a real house like we do. I guess I feel kind of sorry for her. She doesn't have a father, at least none that I know of. Maybe her parents are divorced. Or maybe he died."

"Do you think she's pretty?" I asked, thinking of Sandy's freckled face and brown hair, with bangs that usually need to be trimmed.

"She's very short," said Adele. "She's the smallest person in our class."

"Don't remind me of how small she is," I said, making a face.

"Why?"

"Have you ever noticed anything about her clothes?" I asked.

"Actually, I have," Adele answered. "She's got some good stuff. Some of her sweaters look pretty expensive. Better than you'd expect from someone in the apartments."

"You mean you haven't recognized them?" I asked.

"I'm not as good as you with the names," she reminded me. "I can't tell Ralph Lauren from the Gap. But I do like the things she wears. I wouldn't mind having that slacks outfit she wore yesterday. Did you notice? It was plaid, and she wore it with a shirt that matched one of the stripes in the plaid. And there was a vest, too. In fact, it reminded me of an outfit you used to have."

"Of course I noticed it," I said with disgust. "Anyone with half a brain would recognize it, because it was my old outfit that doesn't fit me anymore. My mom took it to Twice Blessed, and that's where her mom found it."

Adele looked surprised.

"It makes me so angry," I said.

"Why? I don't see what's wrong with her wearing clothing that no longer fits you. And besides, you have loads of new stuff, so why shouldn't Sandy wear the things you can't?"

"Adele," I growled at her. "You sound like my mother. How would you like to see last year's version of yourself every time you walk into school?"

Adele shook her head. "That's a silly way to look at it. You're you and Sandy is Sandy. She looks different from you.

She'd probably love to have your long blond hair and blue eyes. Too bad you can't pick up items like that at a thrift shop."

I had to smile at the image. "I guess she can dye her hair when she gets older," I said. "But it would never look as good as natural blond. Anyway, I wish I could get back at her for embarrassing me by wearing my old clothing."

"Maybe you could ask her not to wear the stuff to school. Only she might not have anything else to wear instead," Adele said.

"Listen," I said, lowering my voice even though we were sitting on the swings in my backyard and no one was around to overhear us. "I've been thinking of a trick to play on Sandy. It's a crazy idea, but I think it would work."

"What is it?" Adele asked curiously.

"I'd thought I'd invite her here for a party," I said. Even as I said it, the plan began to seem better and better. I was sure it would work.

"What kind of a party?" Adele wanted to know.

"I thought I'd print up an invitation on my computer. I'd call it a birthday party. She won't know that my birthday was in February. After all, she wasn't invited when I had my party then."

I went on explaining my idea. "The invitation would say to come to my house for a party on April thirty-first."

"Sounds okay," said Adele somewhat doubtfully. "Only you'll have to pick another date. There is no April thirty-first. But you could have a party on April thirtieth or May first."

"No, no, Adele," I said. "You're missing the whole point. I'm inviting her to a nonexistent party on a nonexistent date. And she won't know when to come."

"If you ask me, that sounds pretty mean," Adele said.

"Maybe so. But I'm feeling mean and angry. Anyhow, it's just a joke. It's no big deal," I added, defending myself.

Just then my mother called out to Adele and me. She was going to the mall and she offered to take us with her. So, being in the car with my mom, we didn't continue talking about the April thirty-first party.

On Monday, I handed Sandy the "invitation," which I'd printed out. "Don't mention it to anyone," I told her. "I'm not inviting a whole lot of people."

Sandy flushed and then smiled at me. For a moment I felt a twinge of guilt, but then I noticed she was wearing my old gray turtleneck sweater. It was knit for me by my grandmother, and just seeing it on Sandy made me angry all over again.

That week, Friday was April thirtieth. Saturday was May first. Adele and I were sitting on the steps outside my house when Sandy arrived on Saturday afternoon. Her mother let her out of their car, which was old and dented. It sounded as if the car could use a new muffler.

"Thanks, Mom," I heard Sandy say as she leaned over to kiss her mother.

"Have fun," a voice responded. And then the car was gone and Sandy was coming up my walk. She was wearing the plaid outfit again, but with a blue shirt that picked out the blue stripe in the plaid. That shirt had once been mine, too. It suddenly occurred to me that if I kept recognizing my old clothes, maybe Sandy did, too. How did she feel about always wearing someone else's old things?

"What are you doing here?" I asked quickly, before I could feel bad about the trick I was playing.

Sandy blushed. "I'm here for your birthday party," she replied. She pulled a piece of paper out of the pocket of my old slacks.

"There's no birthday party," I said. "My birthday was in February."

"Well, what about this invitation?" Sandy asked.

I took the paper and pretended to study it. "This says April thirty-first," I said, looking up from it. "There is no such date. Today's May first." I paused for a moment.

"Ha-ha. I fooled you."

Sandy looked stunned. I thought she was going to cry. But then she took a deep breath and said angrily, "I know there's no April thirty-first. I'm not stupid. But I thought you made a mistake when you printed the date. I didn't know you were just playing a joke on me. *That's* where I was dumb."

"So why aren't you laughing if it's a joke?" I asked her.

"It's not a very funny joke," she said.

I looked at Adele. She was still sitting on the steps and looking very uncomfortable. "How is she going to get home now that her mom's gone?" she asked me.

I hadn't thought about the mile-and-a-half distance between my home and Sandy's.

Sandy put her hand in her pocket and pulled out a small wrapped package. "I guess if it's not your birthday and there's no party, I can keep this gift for myself," she said.

"What is it?" I asked. "Something else you got at the thrift shop? I don't want your secondhand junk."

"As a matter of fact, it is from the thrift store. But like you said, you don't want it." She put the little package back in her pocket.

Sandy started walking down the street.

"Come on back," I called to her. "I want to see what you brought me."

Sandy stopped and shouted at me. "Look," she said. "I fell for your joke, okay? Be satisfied with that. I'm going home."

I thought about the mile-and-a-half walk

she had ahead of her. Adele must have thought about it, too, because she went after Sandy. "Wait. I'll walk part of the way with you."

"We can all walk together," I said, catching up to them.

So there we were, walking down the street together, Adele and me, with Sandy in the middle. For the first block, none of us said anything. But as we waited for the light to change, to cross the street, I grabbed Sandy's arm. "Look. I'm awfully sorry," I said. "I know it was a mean thing to do. But I just wanted to get back at you for coming to school every day wearing my old clothes."

"How do you think I feel?" Sandy responded.

"How do you feel?" Adele asked her.

"I think Mimi wears the most fantastic

clothes. I was thrilled when my mom started bringing her stuff home to me. At first I thought it was just a coincidence. After all, they sold more than one pair of these slacks at the department store. Other people bought them, too. But after the third coincidence in a row, I realized I was dressing up in your clothing from last year. After all, I'm so much smaller than you. I'm just a shrimp."

"Actually, you look very good in Mimi's clothing," Adele said to her.

"It makes me sad to see you wearing my things," I found myself saying. "It reminds me of the past. Lots of times, I went shopping with my grandmother. My grandmother had such good taste. She always found the best bargains and the best colors. We picked out some of my favorite outfits together."

"Mimi's grandmother has Alzheimer's," said Adele. "They can't go shopping to-gether anymore."

"We can't do anything. She doesn't even recognize me," I said, sniffing back tears.

"At least she had a long life and you really got to know her," said Sandy. "My father got sick and died when I was so young, I can hardly remember him," she said. "Listen," she added. "Even if it isn't your birthday, this is yours." She pulled the little package out of her pocket and put it in my hand.

I found a tissue in my pocket and blew my nose. Then I ripped the paper off the package and opened the box. Inside was a silver ring with a garnet.

I gasped. "This is my ring. Where did you get it?"

"It was in the zipper pocket of the down

jacket that you wore last year and I wore this year," Sandy said.

"Why didn't you give it back to me before?" I demanded. "I looked for it everywhere. It belonged to my grandmother. It had been hers when she was my age, and it was the last thing she gave me before her mind went. It's very special to me," I said, trying to put the ring on the finger where I wore it in the past. Then I remembered why I had taken it off. The ring had gotten too tight on my finger and squeezed me.

"My mom bought the jacket at Twice Blessed. The ring in the pocket was like a bonus for me. At least, that's what I told myself. But I never could bring myself to wear it to school because I thought you'd want it back. And then I heard you talking about it one day and I realized that you didn't even know that you'd taken it off and put it in your jacket pocket. I knew I should give it back to you but you were never very friendly to me, so I decided you didn't deserve it. When I thought you were inviting me to your birthday party, I guessed you wanted to be friends with me after all. This seemed to be the perfect time to give you the ring." Sandy stopped for breath. "I was wrong about you wanting to be friends," she said, "but it is your ring. So take it."

"It doesn't even fit me anymore," I complained.

"That's not a problem," said Sandy. "You could put it on a ribbon and wear it around your neck. And someday, when you grow up, you can give it to your daughter. And you can tell her about your grandmother."

Suddenly I found myself crying. Sandy was being so nice to me, and I had been so mean to her. "I'm sorry," I said to her. "I do want to be friends with you."

Sandy looked at me. "Really?" she asked.

"Really, really. Cross my heart and hope to die."

"It's not another joke?" asked Sandy.

"Absolutely not. We can all three be friends together."

And then, because we were near Ben & Jerry's ice-cream store, I felt in my pockets. I had some money on me. It wasn't enough for three ice-cream cones, but my cousin Josh works there on Saturdays. I knew he'd let us buy the ice cream and I could pay him whatever amount I owed later in the day. So we went inside and each selected an outrageous flavor, then ate the ice cream as we slowly walked back to my house. It was like a mini-party, even though it was May first and not April thirty-first.

But even more important, the three of us had a good afternoon together. It was the beginning of a new friendship for each of us. I can hardly believe that I was once so mad at her. All that time, Sandy had me fooled. I really like her. No fooling!

sam and pam

by
matthew
holm

100

101

RRRUUMMBBLE

104

THE END!

Sweetie Bird

· · · · · · · · · · · · · · · · · · · ·

BARBARA ANN PORTE

"Ha! Ha! I fooled you!"

"Ha! Ha! I fooled you!"

"I fooled you!"

"If that fool bird doesn't shut its beak, someone's going to wring its neck for sure. Maybe even me. You'd think Ms. Morelo could at least teach it something else to say. Or at any rate, close her windows."

It was barely summer; everyone's windows were open. Why waste money on air-conditioning in this breezy south shore

Long Island community? My mother was complaining to me. Who else? I was at home—no school until fall. She wasn't the only complainer, either. The whole block was up in arms over that noisy blue-and-yellow red-beaked parrot that had moved in a month or so ago along with its owner, an elderly woman who kept to herself.

Finally, they called a meeting. Not counting Ms. Morelo, the entire street was invited. I went with my mom. "You represent me," my father told us, staying behind, watching television with a can of beer and his cigarettes.

"You're gonna get cancer," I told him.

At that first meeting, they formed a committee. They elected me to go have a talk with Ms. Morelo. "Why not? You're home from school, you don't have a job"—at thirteen,

I was a year shy of being able to get my working papers—"and you get along fine with most people." *Except for my father,* I thought.

"Sure, I'll do it," I said. I figured, worst-case scenario, I'd teach that bird something new to say. Hey, maybe I could get it to whistle. My mom liked *Porgy and Bess. "Summertime, and the living is easy."* She always reminds me that she used to sing me to sleep with that. Then she hums a few bars. "Please, not that again," my father always says.

I told the neighbors, "I bet if I work at it, I can get that bird to sound like a flute."

"See, there, you're using your head. Good girl!" the neighbors said.

The next day, I presented myself at Ms. Morelo's. I stood on the stoop in front of her house and rang the bell. She opened the door. "Yes, girlie?"

Perched on her shoulder, the parrot muttered, "Hey, girlie. Hey, sweetheart." I was shocked.

"I thought he only knew 'I fooled you!'" I said.

Maybe Ms. Morelo didn't hear me. She looked pretty old. Could she be hard of hearing? In that case, she probably never heard the parrot, either.

"Speak up!" she told me. "Are you selling magazines? I already have too many. I don't need anyone to mow the lawn, either. I'm a renter. I say let the grass grow or the landlord can cut it. Either way, it isn't my business."

"Oh, no. I've just come for a visit. I live next door," I told her.

Ms. Morelo squinted. "Right you are," she

said. "I thought you looked familiar. Well, don't just stand there letting in flies. Come on in! Have some lemonade!"

I went in. I sat at the kitchen table while Ms. Morelo set out cookies and poured us each a drink. She added a splash of rum to hers. "It's medicinal," she told me. Then she took one seat, the parrot another. "His name is Ricardo. He's older than I am. Sweetie bird, tell Girlie hello," she told the parrot.

"My name is Joleen," I said.

"My name is Joleen," the parrot echoed. Then, "Ha! Ha! I fooled you!" After which, he ruffled his feathers and squawked very loudly.

"See, he's excited to have company. Usually it's just him and me," said Ms. Morelo.

"I see," I said. Then I moved on to the reason I had come. "Not me, I like parrots myself. It's the neighbors. They think your bird is too noisy. Plus, he's always shouting just that one sentence. It gets on their nerves. I thought maybe I could teach him something new to say. Or maybe a song he could whistle. Something to keep his mind off 'I fooled you!'"

At that moment, louder than ever, that bird screeched his favorite phrase, followed softly by a jumbled monologue. "Pieces of eight, pieces of eight, behind the gate, behind the gate; silver galore, silver galore, behind the door, behind the door; slivers of gold, slivers of gold, down in the hold, down in the hold." Finally, tilting his head and eyeing me with interest, he finished up. "Ha! Ha! I fooled you!"

Wow! Just for a moment, I was speechless. Who knew that any bird could say so much at once? Not to mention, I knew pirate lingo when I heard it. I'd done a school report that spring on piracy. Female pirates in particular interested me. I knew of three: Anne Bonney, Mary Reed, and Ching Shih. Could Ms. Morelo also be one? Or possibly know some?

Trying to be tactful, I said, "These are excellent cookies, Ms. Morelo. Did you bake them yourself? Maybe from some pirate recipe? Handed down to you, perhaps? Are there any pirates in your family?"

"Pirates? Who said anything about pirates? Why are you asking me that?" Possibly disconcerted by the question, or maybe it was the rum, Ms. Morelo spilled her lemonade. Wiping it up, she said, "If you're referring to my dear departed husband's being forced to walk the plank on account of double-dealing, don't you believe it. It was all some cockamamie story invented by the tabloids."

"Don't you believe it! Don't you believe it!" warned the parrot. He pulled out a feather, then shrieked, "Ha! Ha! I fooled you!" It was very annoying to hear that again, yet it reminded me of why I had come in the first place.

"So, Ms. Morelo," I said, "would it be okay with you if I came by every day for a while to practice whistling with Ricardo?" By now, I realized his vocabulary was more than sufficient, and I knew birds didn't need people to *teach* them to whistle, but wouldn't more formal music be a nice change? By way of demonstration, I trilled a few bars of "Summertime."

"Fish are jumping," Ricardo muttered. Then, bobbing his head, he added, "I fooled

you!" Let me tell you, that was one annoying bird.

"Sure, girlie, that would be fine," said Ms. Morelo, who suddenly seemed anxious to be rid of me. Probably she wasn't used to so much company.

Back home, I got busy on the Internet. First I did a Boolean search, linking the terms "piracy" and "Morelo." I knew how to do this from school. Getting nowhere, I tried different names with similar spellings. Still nothing. Next, I went to my public library's online historical news database and searched *it*. Same deal, except I did find a reference to piracy off the coast of Long Island, in Amagansett Bay, in the late fifties and early sixties. Also, although it happened later, there was a reference to an unidentified man overboard whose body was never recovered.

Let's see, I thought. Both Ms. Morelo and Ricardo would have been around back then. I could hardly wait to go back the next day to question her some more.

Heading over the next morning as early as I dared, I warned myself, *Be cool!* I knew from watching my father play poker: Don't show your hand; don't overplay it; know when to call or make a bluff. I formulated my questions carefully. When I arrived, I was ready.

First off, leaving out Amagansett, I said to Ms. Morelo, "So, your husband was a seafaring man?"

"Umm," said Ms. Morelo, her tone noncommital. Perhaps she played poker, too.

Trying to sound offhanded, I made my pitch. "Did your husband know any pirates? Did they drown him on purpose?"

"Partners, not pirates. There's a difference. Accidents happen. I'd think at your age you'd know that," she said.

"Fooled you!" shouted Ricardo.

I took a new tack. "Don't pirates sometimes have parrots? How did you come by Ricardo?"

"He belonged to my father. When my father died, he left him to me."

"Was your father a pirate?"

"Yo—heave-ho, and a bottle of rum!" Ricardo laughed. That's when it occurred to me, I might find out a lot more by interviewing him.

Therefore, addressing Ms. Morelo, I said, "I think Ricardo and I will make better progress if his lesson is private."

"Right," said Ms. Morelo. Leaving us together in the living room, she went into the kitchen. I heard ice cubes clink.

"Medicinal," Ricardo muttered.

"So, what do you do?" I asked him.

"What do you know? Know you so," the parrot said back.

"Pirate treasure?" I asked.

"Treasure pleasure. Pirates to know you," said Ricardo.

From music appreciation in school, I recalled the chorus to a shanty. Hoping to jump-start Ricardo's memory, I whistled some bars.

Ricardo chuckled. "Gold in the hold! Gold in the hold!" he whispered. Then he shouted, "Ha! Ha! I fooled you!"

I seemed to be getting nowhere fast. Still, I wasn't ready to give up. I told Ricardo, "I'll be back tomorrow."

On and off for the rest of the day, I reviewed in my head what I knew about pirates:

Double-dealing, walking the plank, gold in the hold. Or maybe not. Finally, eureka! I asked myself, If gold were in the hold, why would Mr. Morelo have been made to walk the plank? He must have *fooled* them. Put it somewhere else. Weren't pirates known to bury treasure on islands and on coasts? Why not Long Island? Wow!

I came up with a plan. For the next several days, masquerading as a teacher, I visited Ms. Morelo to converse with her bird. He taught me several sea songs with lyrics too rude to repeat. At the end of the week, I approached Ms. Morelo. "Can Ricardo fly?"

"Not now, not much. I keep his flight feathers trimmed so he won't fly off and get lost."

"How long would it take for them to grow back?"

"Not long. Why?"

I played my bluff. I was guessing that the bird had accompanied Mr. Morelo on some of his trips. It seemed more than likely he knew more than he was telling. Therefore, I told Ms. Morelo, "For sure Ricardo knows where your husband hid his treasure. Fear of being forced by pirates to show them or else walk the plank must be why he keeps it to himself. Well, by now, I'm sure all the pirates are dead. But he's just a bird. What does he know? If he could fly, though, he'd be fearless. Plus, he could lead us there."

It wasn't like Ms. Morelo had so much to do at home. An adventure! Why not? "Sure, girlie," she said. "You come back in three weeks, when Ricardo's fully feathered."

Three weeks later to the day, I presented myself at Ms. Morelo's. "Ready?" I said.

"Ready," said Ricardo.

"For what?" asked Ms. Morelo. Then she laughed, picked up her car keys, and said, "Ha! Ha! I fooled you!" She sounded exactly like her bird. Weird.

Meantime, lifting off from his perch, Ricardo circled the room, swooped down, and landed on my head. Very creepy. I mean, it wasn't as if that bird were wearing a diaper. "Gold in the hold. Gold in the hold," he muttered. Did he know something we didn't? Well, wasn't that what we were about to find out?

Ms. Morelo unrolled some string from a spool, tied one end to Ricardo's right leg, removed him from my head, then handed the spool to me. "You can play it out or take it up through the sunroof as you need to," she said. We all three got into her station wagon. Holding Ricardo aloft through the jagged hole in the roof, sounding like a picture-show detective talking to a bloodhound, she told him, "Find treasure!" More softly, she added, "Fly low. Go slow, sweetie bird."

Ricardo did. Ms. Morelo followed after. I controlled the string. Other drivers, concentrating on the road, talking on their cell phones, didn't seem to notice the blue-and-yellow parrot flying overhead, occasionally shouting, "I fooled you!" Neither did the children riding in backseats, eyes glued to Game Boys.

After some time, Ms. Morelo turned in to the parking lot of a nightspot that looked as if it had seen better days. "Well, if that doesn't beat all," she said, pulling up to the entrance and turning off the motor. Ricardo, having by now landed on the car hood, was shifting from foot to foot on account of the heat. He was happy to climb onto Ms. Morelo's arm as soon as he could. By now both she and I were out of the car.

"Where are we?" I asked, handing her the spool of string.

"What's the matter, girlie, can't you read?" she said, pointing toward the neon sign—THE BLUE MERLIN, unlit on account of the daylight.

Just then, a short, chubby man, blue-eyed and balding, came bounding through the doorway, shouting, "For goodness' sake, as I live and breathe, if it ain't Lurleen. I'd know you anywhere."

"Lurleen?" I said. So did Ricardo.

"It was my stage name," Ms. Morelo told me. "Years ago, I used to dance here. It's where I met my husband. Evenings, he'd come off the boat with his boys for dinner."

"I thought you taught kindergarten," I said. That was according to my mother, based on neighborhood scuttlebutt.

"I did. In the daytime I taught kindergarten. At night, I belly danced. When I was young, I had that much energy, believe me."

"Fooled you! Fooled you! Fooled you!" shouted Ricardo.

"I see you still have that fool bird," said the man. *"Buenos días, Ricardo."*

"Buenos días," Ricardo said back. Wow! Who would have imagined a bilingual bird?

Ms. Morelo introduced us. "This here is Joleen. Joleen, meet Sam Lavine, my former boss and my husband, Moey's, best friend."

"You sure know how to lay low," Mr. Lavine said. "After Moey's accident, I looked for you for a long time. He left something for you. 'If something bad happens to me, see Lurleen gets this,' he told me. Ever since, it's been in my storeroom."

"What is it?" Ms. Morelo asked.

"It's a trunk. What's inside I don't know. I'm not nosy. Whatever it is, though, I'm sure that it's safe. My storeroom is climate controlled. It's as good as a humidor."

What's a humidor? I wondered. And why did Mr. Lavine wink?

With Ricardo on her shoulder, Ms. Morelo and I followed him past the bar, then into the storeroom, which he unlocked. The air was pleasantly cool and sweet-smelling. Mr. Lavine switched on a light. Hidden behind bottles of wine, covered with a dirty canvas sheet and torn sailcloth, was a wooden trunk. "I'll leave you alone with your treasure," Mr. Lavine said, exiting the room.

Surprisingly agile for her age, Ms. Morelo knelt, undid the trunk clasps, and raised the lid. The aroma grew sweeter. She inhaled deeply. Giving an excited squawk, Ricardo raced down her arm, reached one foot into the trunk, and lifted out a long, dark, pencil-like object. *"Cohiba, cohiba, cohiba,"* he chortled gleefully. He held it to his beak.

"A cigar? Does Ricardo smoke?" I asked.

"Silly girl," Ms. Morelo said. "Smoking is bad for anyone's health. Ricardo is sniffing. He was raised on my family's *finca,* a tobacco farm in Cuba. He knows treasure when he smells it. A Cuban cigar is like money in your hand. A trunkful's a fortune. Well, properly aged and stored, like this, in a room like a humidor." Then Ms. Morelo stood and went to find Sam so he could help load the trunk into her station wagon.

"Don't be a stranger. Come back soon, now, you hear?" he called after us as we drove off. Did he also mean me? From inside the car, Ricardo was shouting, "Ha! Ha! I fooled you!" His old trick. Possibly to sidetrack any pirates still lurking? I wondered. Well, the morning's events had given me plenty to think about.

Almost home, Ms. Morelo said, "Okey dokey, here's the story, the whole megillah, no hanky-panky. My Moey was a businessman, a commodities trader. After a haul, he'd tell me, 'Hey, I'm only getting back for you what's rightfully yours.' He meant on account of my family's cigar business, nationalized under Castro in Cuba, and Cuban cigars outlawed here.

But in the end, see what it got him—dealing with criminals."

"Hanky-panky," said Ricardo.

"Pirates?" I asked.

"Who knows? Smugglers for sure. Girlie, don't you ever do that," said Ms. Morelo.

"No," I said. "I won't."

As it happened, a block meeting was scheduled for the following night. The neighbors would want a progress report. They were sure to ask, "So, why is that parrot still shouting, 'I fooled you!'" What would I tell them? Should I rat on Ms. Morelo, turn her in for harboring illegal booty? What would happen to her and Ricardo? But if I kept mum, wouldn't that make me an accomplice to a crime? All that day and night, I worried what to do.

In the morning, I went next door to tell

Ms. Morelo that I'd decided to take her advice and not get mixed up with criminals. Either she had to turn herself in or I'd have to. I rang the bell. Nobody answered. Peering through the glass entranceway panel, I saw that the house looked vacated. I walked toward the back. The station wagon was gone. About to leave, I noticed something sticking up out of the mailbox. It was a brown paper bag with my name on it. Inside was a cigar, and a note: "To Joleen, a souvenir to thank you for your help. Don't you smoke it!"

Well, that night, I told the neighbors everything. No one believed me. "That's some story," they told one another. "She's going to grow up to be a writer for sure." They didn't care. They were all just glad that the parrot was gone.

• • •

Years have gone by. The neighbors were correct. I did grow up to be a writer. Still, when I look back on that summer, I wonder, *Did all that really happen? Which parts did I make up?* If only I could find Ms. Morelo and Ricardo to ask them.

I hunt up my Cuban cigar—stale now, and crumbled—and the note: "Don't you smoke it!" Well, of course not. How unhealthy!

The Bridge to Highlandsville

· · · · · · · · · · · · · · · · · ·

MICHELLE KNUDSEN

Prince Everett was a very, very, *very* important person. At least, he thought so. And since his opinion was the only one he actually cared about, that was all that mattered.

He was on a very important journey. Of course, any journey he was on would automatically be important, just because it involved him, but this one was *especially* important. He was on his way to Highlandsville. There was some sort of situation going on there. A dragon, a princess, something about a rescue and reward. He was a little fuzzy on the details, but it was just the kind of thing that could earn him fame and fortune and a well-deserved place in the history books. Then everyone would know exactly how important a person he really was.

Right now, people didn't really seem to get it.

Take the innkeeper from last night, for example. He had simply refused to understand that Everett could not be expected to sleep in the loft above the stables. And it wasn't the first time that had happened. Perhaps, you might say, innkeepers were, as a rule, just a bit thickheaded. But no, Everett had suffered a distressing lack of respect from several people he had met since beginning this adventure. Nearly everyone, in fact. Especially the innkeeper's wife, who had demanded their horses as payment after that little accident with the fire and the venison stew. But no matter. Once Everett completed his journey to Highlandsville and did the . . . the thing—rescued the dragon and slew the princess or whatever—everything would be different.

"Right, Otto?" he asked. Otto was the swordsman he'd brought along to handle any actual fighting that might occur. Everett was far too important to deal with that sort of thing himself, of course.

"What's right, Boss?" asked Otto.

Everett sighed. "Can't you just agree? If I say something's right, it's right. When I say, 'Right, Otto?' you just say, 'Right, Boss!' Is that so difficult?"

"But how can I say 'Right' if I don't know what I'm saying 'Right' to?"

Everett shook his head. "Never mind, Otto. Let's just keep walking."

After a minute, Otto said, "I wish we still had our horses."

That afternoon, they came to a high bridge across a wide river.

"Finally!" said Everett. "The bridge to Highlandsville."

They started across, Otto peering nervously down at the rushing water far below. Suddenly, a medium-size but enormously ugly creature swung up from under the bridge and planted itself firmly in the center, blocking the way.

"Toll, please," it said.

"Toll?" said Everett. "What toll?"

"Bridge toll," said the creature.

"That's preposterous," said Everett. "I'm not paying any toll. Get out of my way. It's very important that I get to Highlandsville at once."

"Uh, Boss," began Otto, "I don't think you should—"

But Everett wasn't listening. He strode forward, intending to brush right past the creature without a second glance. Before he had taken two steps, however, the creature began to grow. It expanded to fill the entire width of the bridge and then some, its lumpy skin spilling out over the railing and its now-giant head looming up high above even Otto, who was generally considered rather tall.

"Toll, please," it boomed down at them, frowning malevolently.

"Gah," said Everett, staring up in dismay. He felt Otto's beefy finger tap him on the shoulder.

"Boss?" said Otto softly. "I don't think

we should try to cross without paying the toll."

"Gah," said Everett, nodding. Together they backed slowly off the bridge.

The creature shrank abruptly down to its former less-threatening size and sat in the middle of the bridge, waiting.

After a minute, when his heart was no longer beating quite so fast, Everett took a step forward.

"Now, look here, you," he began.

"Toll, please," said the creature.

"Uh, yes. All right, what is this toll?" Everett asked.

"Three things," said the creature.

Everett waited. "Did you have some particular things in mind?" he asked, finally. "Or just any three things?"

The creature narrowed its eyes at him briefly. Then it said, "These three things:

"A pretty red flower whose leaves won't bend,

A twelve-line poem by your own hand penned,

And a furry brown puppy, to be my little friend."

There was a brief, uncomfortable silence.

"Seriously?" Everett asked. *"That's* the toll?"

The creature nodded.

Everett sighed. "Look, you, uh—"

"Troll," said the creature. "Toll troll."

"Uh, yes. All right. Listen, is this really necessary? I don't have time to run around and fetch things for you. I must get to High-landsville. Couldn't we just give you some gold, and—"

"No."

"But with gold, you could—"

"No."

"But if you just—"

"No."

"Uh, Boss," said Otto quickly, "let's not make him angry again, okay?"

Everett looked at the troll. The troll made itself about three inches bigger.

"All right, then," said Everett. "Fine. We'll pay the toll." He turned and strode away from the bridge, leaving Otto to hurry after him.

As soon as they were out of sight and earshot of the bridge, Everett found a relatively clean stone without too many sharp pointy parts and sat down to think. There had to be some way to get around this toll business.

"Hey, Boss?"

"Not now, Otto."

"But I was thinking—for that first thing, what if we painted a flower on a rock or something? Then the leaves wouldn't bend, right?"

"Otto, I said—" Everett paused. "That's actually a pretty good idea."

Otto grinned. "Thanks, Boss!"

"Yes. We'll give the troll that, make it think we're going to play along . . ."

Otto stopped smiling. "Make him think? I don't understand. Those other toll things aren't so hard to get. Why don't we just give him what he wants?"

"Because it's ridiculous. I'm not running around on the whim of some deluded creature who thinks it owns the bridge. I'm too im—I mean, we have important things to do."

Otto frowned. "But it would probably be quicker just to—"

Everett reached into his pocket and brought out some of their little remaining gold. "Here. Go and get some paint and do your rock idea. I need to think."

"Okay, Boss." Otto took the gold and tramped off toward the last town they'd passed through.

Everett nodded to himself. It was going to be fine. This was just a little obstacle; nothing he couldn't handle. He could think of it as a warm-up for the main event. First a troll, then a dragon. Or princess. Or whatever. It made total sense.

Otto returned in about an hour, carrying a large sack. He placed it on the ground and removed some red and green paint and a little brush. Then he took out some paper and ink and a quill.

"I got you some paper for the poem," he

said. "Did you think of something good to write?"

"I'm not going to write a poem," Everett said. "You'll see, it will be fine. Paint your rock."

Otto found a small flat rock and painted a surprisingly lovely red flower on its surface. Everett took a nap while Otto worked. As soon as the paint was dry, they headed back toward the bridge.

"Just keep quiet and follow my lead," Everett whispered.

"Okay, Boss," said Otto unhappily.

"Troll!" Everett called. "We have your items!"

The troll bounded into view from under the bridge. "Toll, please?" it asked hopefully.

"Yes, yes, the toll. Here's the flower, first." He walked forward and placed the stone on the bridge surface, then quickly backed away. The troll bounced forward and snatched up the rock, peering at it skeptically. Then suddenly it grinned. "Leaves won't bend!" it exclaimed. Otto beamed.

"Yes, you see? We're doing as you asked," Everett said. "Now let us cross, and we'll give you the other items on the farside."

The troll stopped grinning. "Pay toll first," it said.

"But—"

The troll frowned and started to grow. "Toll, please."

"Boss . . ." said Otto urgently.

They backed quickly away. "All right, fine," Everett said. "Wait there—we'll be right back."

They walked back to where they'd left the supplies.

"Do you want me to go find the puppy while you work on the poem?" Otto asked.

"No," said Everett. "We're not getting it a puppy."

"But—"

"Just sit there and be quiet!" Everett snapped. "I need to write this stupid thing."

Luckily, the troll had not said anything about the poem being a good one. Everett wrote:

This is a poem I wrote for a troll.
It's part of some kind of ridiculous toll.
He sits on his bridge and he makes his
    demands.
Won't listen to reason; instead he expands
    and gets bigger and uglier, nasty and
    mean.
Someone should rip out his soft little
    spleen.

I'm very important. I've got things to do.
If you don't believe me, ask Otto—
  it's true!
I do not have patience for poems and
  trolls,
for flowers and puppies and rigamaroles.
I do not enjoy having wasted my day.
I am Prince Everett. Get out of my way.

Everett chuckled as he read the poem over to himself. Otto looked up from where he sat painting flowers on all the nearby rocks.

"Finished, Boss? Can I see?"

Everett handed the paper to Otto and stood up, stretching the crick in his lower back. Ignoring Otto's quickly falling expression, he looked around thoughtfully.

"Uh, Boss, do you really think this is, uh—"

"Quiet. I'm trying to think," Everett said. He was not going to get a puppy for that creature. How could he trick the troll into thinking he was giving it a puppy without actually doing so? His eye fell on the sack Otto had carried the supplies in.

"Otto," Everett said. "Find a puppy-size rock and put it inside that sack."

"Yes, Boss," Otto said sadly. He got up and began searching. When he found an appropriately sized rock, he placed it in the sack and handed it to Everett. Everett immediately marched off toward the bridge with the poem in one hand and the sack in the other. Otto trailed forlornly behind him.

"Troll!" Everett called when they reached the bridge. "Here are the other items!"

The troll reappeared. Everett had Otto carry the poem over to the creature. Its eyes narrowed dangerously as it read, but when the troll looked up again, it only said, "Twelve-line poem, own hand penned," then nodded grudgingly.

"Excellent," said Everett. "And here is your puppy." He held up the sack. The troll took a few little hopeful hops forward. Everett leaned back slightly and whispered to Otto out of the corner of his mouth. "Be ready to run across the bridge," he said.

Then he threw the sack over the railing and down toward the water below.

"PUPPY!" wailed the troll, diving after it.

"Now!" shouted Everett. He tore across the bridge. He could hear Otto's heavy boots pounding quickly just behind him.

They reached the far end and kept running until they seemed a safe distance from the edge of the bridge. Everett turned around just in time to see the wet, angry troll climbing back up over the railing. It held the rock and the sack in its hand.

"Ha!" Everett called triumphantly. "I fooled you! There was no puppy! And you see, we have crossed your bridge regardless! We have made it to Highlandsville! Ha-ha-ha-ha-ha!"

Otto didn't say anything.

The troll looked at Everett silently. Then, it began to laugh. Its mouth grew large and wide, and it laughed great booming laughs for what had to be a full minute. Everett frowned. This was not the response he'd expected. Where was the defeated acknowledgment of his cleverness? Where was the respect he deserved?

"What?" he said finally. "What's so funny? Why are you laughing? I demand that you tell me why you are laughing, Troll!"

The troll's laughter broke down into smaller chuckles until it was only smiling a large and wicked smile. Then it spoke.

"Fooled me. Yes. But fooled you, too."

"What do you mean?" asked Everett. "Fooled me? How?"

The troll's grin widened even farther.

"This is not the bridge to Highlandsville."

Everett blinked. "I beg your pardon?"

The troll leaned forward and spoke very slowly. "Not Highlandsville," it said. "Wrong bridge."

Everett looked around. "This . . . this is not Highlandsville?"

"No," said the troll.

"Well, then, where is Highlandsville?" Everett demanded.

The troll's grin widened a few more inches, stretching the very limits of its lumpy head. Then it raised its hand and pointed.

Everett groaned. Otto made a sound behind him that sounded suspiciously like quickly muffled snickering.

The troll was pointing back in the opposite direction. Back the way they'd come.

Back across the bridge.

"Toll, please."

The Prince of Humbugs

· · · · · · · · · · · · · · · · ·

ELLEN KLAGES

Bethel Village was small, settled by farmers and hatmakers who worked six days a week and spent half the Sabbath in church. Life was hard, and pleasures few, except when the town wags—jokesters and storytellers—gathered in the tavern at the edge of the town green, trying to outdo one another.

On a steamy afternoon in early July, Uncle Phin, the boldest of the tricksters, was at his usual table in the back corner, in the midst of a long and improbable story, when his nephew ran into the tavern, blinking, half-blinded by the bright summer sun.

"It's a boy!" he called out before he'd even reached the table.

Uncle Phin, a round-faced man with a mop of ginger hair, turned to his companions. "The end of that story will have to wait, my friends. It seems I have my first grandchild. Grand*son*." He sounded very proud.

"What is he to be called?" he asked the panting boy.

"They've named him after you, sir."

"Excellent. Excellent." He leaned back in his seat, sounding even more proud than before. "Well, if he's to be a chip off *this* old block, I must give him a suitable gift for his christening. What should it be?" He thought for a moment, then snapped his fingers.

"I have it! I will give him the most valuable thing I own. I'll sign over the deed to my five acres on Ivy Island. He'll be the richest lad in town—that's what I'll tell him."

The baby grew into a sturdy snub-nosed boy. He shared both his grandfather's round face and his name, which was rather long, so the youngster was called Taylor—Tale to his friends. Once school was out and chores were done, he loved to sit on the old man's knee and listen to his clever stories. Sometimes other men tried to best him, but rarely succeeded. Tale was proud that his grandfather's stories were the ones remembered and retold. The seacoast was but a half-day's journey, and Uncle Phin traded goods with sailors there, returning to the village with far-flung yarns of fearsome creatures. Tale's imagination filled with mermaids and sea serpents from the briny deep.

"You're a wealthy boy, with a grand estate," his grandfather would often tell him. "When you come of age, you'll be able to travel to these places and see such marvels for yourself."

A life of adventure beckoned—someday. Tale could barely wait. He endured his school lessons, and the endless chores of a small farm—herding the cows, carrying in firewood, and shucking corn. His parents often had to shout to stir him from his daydreams of riches and wonders to come.

Why should I have to muck out stalls, Tale wondered, *when I am the richest boy in the village? I own the whole of Ivy Island.*

Ivy Island. The thought of it delighted

him, day and night. As Tale grew, his grandfather told him more of the grandeur he would see when he was old enough to take possession of his property. His mother advised him to learn his sums so that he could manage his fortune wisely, and although little else of school held his attention, figures seemed to dance across his slate.

Finally, on his tenth birthday, he could stand it no longer. "Father," he said at supper, "I want to see my inheritance. I want to go to Ivy Island."

His father thought for a long moment before answering. "All right," he said. "We're low on hay, and there's a meadow half a mile from your holdings. If you'll help with the mowing and cutting tomorrow, I'll have one of the hired men take you at the noon break." He paused and looked at his son with a smile. "But you must give me your word that you'll not get a swelled head once you see the fine gift your grandfather has given you."

Tale promised, and barely slept a wink all that night. At dawn he set off with the men and the wagons, and worked as hard as anyone under the hot sun, cutting the hay with a sharp scythe and bundling sheaves with thick twine.

Would noon never come? Tale wondered. The sun seemed to barely creep across the sky, slow as molasses.

When his father called for the dinner break, Tale gave a whoop, and the men stopped and lay down their tools. They sat in the shade of the wagon and uncovered their dinner buckets. Tale wolfed his beans and corn bread in short order. "Can

I go to Ivy Island now?" he asked before his mouth was empty.

His father nodded at an Irishman named Edmund, who downed the last of his cider and shouldered his ax. "All right, then, lad. I suppose it's high time you saw for yourself. Come along with you."

They walked through the field of half-mown hay. At the north end of the meadow, the dry ground began to grow damp. Tale had to leap from hummock to dry hummock to avoid soaking his pants and boots. But meadow soon became bog, and Tale slipped, arms flailing, sinking up to his waist in moss and brackish water. It stank of decaying plants and covered him in a slippery gray-green muck.

"Just a quarter mile to go," Edmund said cheerfully.

Only the promise of Ivy Island, his very own paradise on the other side of this dismal swamp, allowed Tale to gather his strength and wade on. Fifteen minutes later, sopping wet, covered in mud and mosquito bites, Tale stood once again on dry land, on the bank of a burbling creek.

"There it is," said Edmund. "The gateway to your fame and fortune." His voice sounded as if it promised gold and jewels and long-lost treasure. With two swings of his ax, he cut down a small oak, which fell across the creek and formed a crude bridge.

"Step right up, young man, and behold the wonders of Ivy Island," he said with a smile.

Tale crossed the oak bridge carefully but quickly.

Ivy Island. At last.

He stood on his property and looked around. This side of the island was shadowed by scraggly trees twined with pale stunted ivy. Poison ivy. *A natural barrier, to protect the rich farmland beyond from prying, envious eyes,* Tale thought. He walked inland, but the landscape did not change. The ground was spongy, and the leaves of the trees hung thin and yellowed.

A long black snake slithered from under a rock, its head raised.

"Well, well. I believe that's one of your tenants." Edmund chuckled.

Tale stopped and stared at the hired man, then turned and looked in all directions. This was his fortune? His estate? His shoulders slumped. The land was worthless. Barren and surrounded on all sides by nearly impassable swamp.

"No! No, no, no," Tale whispered. *There must be some mistake.*

But he watched Edmund smile and whistle all the way back to the hay wagon, and when they arrived, Tale saw that his father and the other men were laughing, too. He stood stock-still, mud-covered and downcast.

Everyone had known. For ten years—his entire life—his family, his neighbors, the whole village, had been in on the joke. His grandfather's joke. Ivy Island was just another one of his clever stories, no more real than a mermaid.

Tale said nothing for the rest of the afternoon. He kept his head down and did not look at his father or any of the other men. He swung the scythe and mowed the stalks of hay as if they were an enemy army.

When the wagon returned to the village, Tale leaped off and, without stopping to clean himself up, ran straight to the tavern. It seemed that everyone was out on the green that day, and each person he passed had the same greeting.

"Tale! Taylor! I hear you've been to Ivy Island," each one said. They smiled; they chuckled; they laughed out loud. It was as if there was a village fair, a rare afternoon of fun and amusement, and everyone had been invited except him.

The boy dashed into the tavern, away from the merriment that reddened his face more than a day in the summer sun. But inside the dim room, it was worse. Laughter echoed off the wooden walls. Men raised their tankards to him in mocking toasts.

"Ah, here he is. All hail the sovereign lord of Ivy Island."

Tale stared at the wet prints his sodden boots left on the planked floor as he

walked to Uncle Phin's table in the far corner of the room.

"I've been to Ivy Island, Grandfather," he
said.

"And now you know. I fooled you," he
said, nodding.

"Yes. But, but—*why*?" The question
almost tore itself out of Tale's throat.

The older man patted the seat next to
him, and after a long minute, Tale sat.

"You are my first and favorite grandchild,
and you bear my name. And so I wanted
to give you my finest gift, a gift that you
could profit from your whole life."

"Your finest gift?" the boy said, anger
in his voice now. "Five acres of worthless
swamp?"

"The land is not the gift," Phineas Taylor
said softly. "It's the delight on the faces of
the people outside."

"They were laughing at me."

"Well, well, well. Imagine that. A whole village, laughing on an ordinary afternoon? Now *there's* something you don't see every day." He put an arm around the boy's shoulder. "Life is hard. People need to be amused, astounded, even tricked from time to time. A good humbug lightens their steps, takes their minds off their troubles. The man who can pull that off has a rare gift, a skill he can use anywhere in the wide world."

P. T. Barnum stared at his grandfather for a long moment.

"Thank you," he said, and began to smile.

About the Authors

. . .

DAVID A. ADLER is the author of more than two hundred books for young readers, including the Cam Jansen series; the Young Cam Jansen books; the Picture Book Biography series, about such diverse subjects as Benjamin Franklin, Martin Luther King Jr., Helen Keller, and Anne Frank; and the award-winning picture books *The Babe & I* and *Lou Gehrig: The Luckiest Man.* His most recent work is a novel for older readers, *Don't Talk to Me About the War.* David lives on Long Island, New York, with his wife. They have three grown sons and two grandsons.

• • •

DOUGLAS FLORIAN is known for his illustrations as well as his poetry. His books include *Beast Feast, Insectlopedia, A Pig Is Big, Zoo's Who,* and *Summersaults.* Doug has also illustrated covers for *The New Yorker* magazine and exhibited his art in New York City galleries. He and his wife live on Long Island, New York, with their five children.

• • •

EVE B. FELDMAN was born in New York, has lived in Israel and Iran, and currently lives on Long Island. She is the author of *Seymour, the Formerly Fearful; Dog Crazy; and That Cat!;* as well as the picture books *Animals Don't Wear Pajamas* and *Birthdays!* Her newest title is the picture book *Billy & Milly, Short & Silly.*

• • •

MATTHEW HOLM is the illustrator of the graphic novel series Babymouse, which is written by his older sister, Jennifer Holm. According to his website, he claims to "sit around and draw pictures of mice all day." For this book, he took time off to draw a pair of chimpanzees. He lives in Portland, Oregon, with his wife and their dog and ferret.

• • •

JOHANNA HURWITZ grew up in New York City, where many of her books take place. These include The Riverside Kids series, the Ali Baba Bernstein books, and the Park Pals adventures. She is also the author of the Class Clown series and, most recently, the Monty books. She and her husband divide the year between Long Island and Vermont. They have two grown children, three grandchildren, and one cat.

• • •

ELLEN KLAGES was born in Ohio and now lives in San Francisco. Her first novel, *The Green Glass Sea,* won the Scott O'Dell Award for historical fiction, the Judy Lopez Memorial Award for Children's Literature, and the New Mexico Young Adult Book

Award. The sequel, *White Sands, Red Menace,* was published in the fall of 2008. Her stories have been translated into Czech, German, French, Swedish, and Japanese, and she recently published a collection of stories for adults called *Portable Childhoods,* which includes the Nebula Award–winning story "Basement Magic."

. . .

MICHELLE KNUDSEN is the author of more than forty books for children, including the *New York Times* bestselling picture book *Library Lion* and the middle-grade fantasy novel *The Dragon of Trelian.* Formerly a full-time children's book editor, she has also worked as a freelance editor, bookseller, substitute teacher, library supervisor, and managing editor, among other things. She lives in Brooklyn, New York.

. . .

CARMELA A. MARTINO is a freelance writer and writing teacher. She writes for both children and adults. Her first children's novel, *Rosa, Sola,* was named to *Booklist* magazine's "Top Ten First Novels for Youth: 2006." Her most recent publications include a poem in *Chicken Soup for the Soul: Teens Talk High School,* and an article in the *2010 Children's Writers and Illustrator's Market.* She recently cofounded a group blog with five other teaching authors to share writing tips and exercises for writers of all ages. Carmela grew up in Chicago in a bilingual household, speaking Italian and English. A lifelong Cubs fan, she now cheers the team on from her home in Naperville, Illinois, along with her husband and son.

• • •

MEGAN McDONALD is the youngest of five sisters. From events in her childhood, she has devised her two well-known series: the Judy Moody books and a companion series about Judy's brother, Stink, as well as a new series, the Sisters Club books. She is also the author of the Julie books in the American Girls series. Megan lives in Sebastopol, California.

• • •

BARBARA ANN PORTE is originally from New York City. She is the author of the many easy readers about Harry, as well as the picture books *Black Elephant with a Brown Ear (in Alabama)* and *Chickens! Chickens!* For older readers, she has written *Something Terrible Happened, I Only Made Up the Roses,* and many other books. Formerly Chief of Children's Services Division for the Nassau Library System, Barbara Ann now lives in Arlington, Virginia, with her husband.